PENNY DOCTORS

Daniel Costello

Copyright © 2016 Daniel Costello
All rights reserved
First Edition

PAGE PUBLISHING, INC.
New York, NY

First originally published by Page Publishing, Inc. 2016

ISBN 978-1-68289-815-4 (pbk)
ISBN 978-1-68289-816-1 (digital)

Printed in the United States of America

The story you are about to read and enjoy is true. Sometime in the early 1920s, a group of "local doctors" came up with an "experiment" they hoped would lead to helping people who were suffering from various diseases. The area we are talking about (small town in Wisconsin) is of lower to lower-middle class, hardworking families. The idea the "doctors" had was to actually kidnap young people, experiment on them in the "local hospital" run by these doctors; and what happened to these residents after will keep you spellbound. Just imagine a father and mother, one day, faced with the reality that their son or daughter is missing and may be in the hands of these "evil doctors" and not knowing what they have planned for them. Eerie. Diabolical. Just wait.

Yes, you ask—can this be true? Even back then, you were not as safe as you might think. Yes, there were "crazies" as there are today, certain types of people who would stop at nothing in order to fulfill their fantasies. Uncaring, ruthless, cunning, the work of the devil himself.

You will find that in the end many times, there is grief and heartache when dealing with science, especially this form of science these doctors have perpetrated upon the young and innocent. As you read this story, just think about how you would react to this happening to you and your family. A good read for a stormy night. Do you know where your children are?

DEDICATION

Family is the cornerstone of happiness and I dedicate this work to my great-granddaughter Lila Willow and thank God for that blessing.

CHAPTER 1

The night was thick with fog. The streets were bare. A small town in Wisconsin, 1923, and like most America were bedded down for the night. During these times with no TV and few radios, there wasn't much to do but read, get ready for the next day, and go to bed.

Homes were quiet unlike the homes of today. Take the Benson family: dad, mom, and three children—two girls and one boy. Ages for the girls were fifteen and twelve while the boy was just turning eighteen. Now, the girls were normal young ladies, but unfortunately, the young boy, Adam, a normal young boy, who was out of school, was looking to maybe join his dad in the tailor shop as so many young men did as college was not always an opportunity.

Getting back to the girls, the fifteen-year-old was named Sarah, and her sister named Rebecca. Girls at that age even with a brother didn't, as a rule, find time or patience for their brother as siblings go. Such is life, then and now.

The father, we'll call him Charles and the mother, Anna. Both parents came from strict upbringing with hardworking parents with religious beliefs. Charles worked during the day at the local tailor shop while Anna was a stay-at-home mom as most women did in the days. Not being able to have Adam placed in college, Anna's chores at home were difficult just trying to deal with and care for her children whom she so dearly loved.

Approximately twenty-five miles away on the other side of town was the only "medical" facility for that area, Bradford General, and in town, one doctor who just about keep up with all the patients. If you had a car, one didn't run to the hospital, so you settled for Dr. Reed, an elderly gentleman with real old-school methods, who really didn't have the time to catch up so called modern medicine. "Take an aspirin and call me in the morning" kind of cure all.

It worked for most. But as we know, people did not live to the ripe old age we do today. In those days, maybe the late forties or early fifties was your limit. That's just the way it was. If you got sick, parents, you dealt with it the best you could, and if one of the children became sick and couldn't afford the local doctor, the next best thing was the "drugstore" in town where Mr. Schneider cared for your ills. Thanks to prayers and some old-fashioned remedies; many times it worked out. Time heals, this they had.

CHAPTER 2

Fulton Street was just your "how would you say" something you'd find in everyday America. Tree lined up, quiet, well-kept homes with lower-, middle-income families. Hardworking folks with an income of probably $2,500.00 with hopes their children would do better. Unlike today, the family gathered around the dinner table each night—not just Sunday and broke bread together.

Mom and Dad at each end of the table, with the girls one side, and Adam, opposite. As usual, the dinner served by the daughters, which was prepared by Mom, lending a hand to kind of give Mom a break. Adam sat quietly as usual. Being old-fashioned, the Benson family sat and enjoyed their meal without much conversation.

Adam, to the surprise of all, spoke first, and yes they all listened. "Mom," he always started that way, "as I was coming home, you know the way I do, honest, Mom, I heard this car behind me, and it stopped right next to me . . . really. I was scared, so I kept walking and they followed.

"Do you need a ride, young man?" they asked.

Adam, the father, shouted, "How many times have we told you do not talk to strangers?" and left it at that.

"Dad . . . please, the men talked to me, and I was scared. That car was scary, and I didn't know what to do, Dad."

"What do you mean? What did the car look like, Adam?"

"Well, it was big and black, and like the one grandma was in last year when she went to heaven and I just don't know. Leave me alone!"

At that point, dinner was over. We all retired early that night trying to ponder what had happened to Adam that day. Not like him to be so upset.

As we lay in bed that night, I turned and looked at my wife, who so dearly loved her son hugged her to assure her no harm would ever come to Adam.

CHAPTER 3

The night drew long. Thinking about what had occurred with Adam that day. I felt bad the way I responded to Adam. But he was a difficult child.

Anna, by this time, had fallen asleep. I quietly got up and went downstairs and decided to go out on the porch for a smoke. It was a beautiful sky, with unbelievable amount of stars and a full moon. As I sat there, I pondered again what Adam had told us and did he make this up for attention—I don't know.

It was about 2:00 a.m.; the night was still. The street was quiet, especially at this time of night in a small rural town. Then I heard what sounded like a car coming down the road and as anyone would wait to see who or what it was.

As the car approached, I stood up and was a little taken aback. It was a large black vehicle just as Adam had told us about earlier that day. As I went out to the street to get a better look, it accelerated out of sight. I sat there for about two more hours, but no other vehicles were to be seen. I retired to bed trying not to wake Anna. Would explain what had happened that night in the morning.

I awoke that morning to the sounds of Anna, as usual, working in the kitchen preparing breakfast. When the children had gone off to school, I would try and tell her, without alarming her the experience I had that evening after we had gone to bed.

"Anna, that was a wonderful breakfast. You never fail to satisfy the hunger, be it breakfast, lunch, or dinner. What would we do without you? Thanks to you!"

As for me telling her about last night, I kept tossing it around in my head and trying to make sense of it. Would this upset Anna? And what if we were all overacting?

"Anna, come here and have another cup of coffee with me. Let's talk."

CHAPTER 4

As a rule, I usually try and get to the tailor shop around 8:30 a.m. to get things in order. But this morning I planned to be late, knowing I had to let Anna know what was going on.

In those days, you just couldn't afford to stay home—money was tight. How was I going to tell Anna what I saw that night without upsetting her too much? She was so close to Adam and the thought of any harm that may come to him would be too hard to bear. Was I overacting to all of this? Should I tell her? Questions, questions, and decisions to make.

Maybe the girls could help. They were streetwise to some extent. This was the 1920s, and people have become more astute and more aware of their surroundings than when Anna and I were growing up. Were we to protect me of Adam? Anna looked at me and asked if I was okay.

Drifting in thought. I responded, "Anna why do you ask?"

"You seem preoccupied," Anna said.

A bit on the defensive I replied, "Nothing I can't handle" and left the kitchen without saying a word.

On the way out the door, I thought, "Don't leave Anna thinking 'what's with Charles' it's not like him."

"Anna," I called, "come here. I'm sorry, just trust in me for now and I'll try and come home early. We'll talk, you and me and the girls. It'll be okay."

"I don't understand, Charles. What will be okay?"

"The incident with Adam yesterday? You know the 'black car' that followed him. Just do me a favor watch for Adam after school. I told him you'd be there, okay?"

CHAPTER 5

I left for work that morning with an ill feeling. Not just for Adam and what had occurred, but for Anna and how she'd react if, say someone did try and bring any harm to her son.

The day seemed to last so long. I couldn't call Anna as we couldn't afford the luxury of having a phone with three children to raise and all. Close the shop early or better yet, just surprise Anna and go home for lunch.

Usually, I just had a sandwich at the back of the shop, in between customers as the walk home was so time consuming and didn't use the car; only when really needed too. Gas was costly those days, it was around eight to ten cents a gallon, and the economy was just recovering from WW1 and jobs were few to find. Having a shop of my own was a plus to say the least.

Back at home on a dismal cloudy day, Anna was sitting in the kitchen pondering all that was going on. She sat there with a cup of tea, some oatmeal cookies she had just finished baking, and in silence, said her daily prayers. "God is good and I know he will help. He has in the past." Faith—yes, faith is a good thing.

The house was so quiet and for some strange reason seemed unsettling. I'm always by myself during the day and comfortable with my surroundings, but not today. As I sat there, the sound of a car outside interrupted my thoughts. I went to the front parlor window and peeked out the curtains.

"Oh," I thought out loud, "there's that car Adam and Charles had mentioned parked in front with the engine going. Who could it be?" I asked myself. "What if they came to the door?

I was alone and at this point became very frightened. I looked at the clock, and it was around the time Adam would be coming home from school. I had to do something, but what to do? I keep peeking through the curtains for Adam and then I heard the doorbell. The black car was still there. "Oh dear god help me," and just then I could see down the street Adam coming home.

The bell rang again and again and again. I went to the door, opened it, and it was Adam's friend. The car drove away.

CHAPTER 6

Adam's friend was comfortable while I patiently awaited Adam to come down the street safe within my sight.

"Benjamin," Adam's friend, I asked, "how about you and I go outside take a walk to meet Adam coming home from school"?

"Yes," answered Ben. Everyone called him Ben for short. "That would be nice Ms. Benson.

"Thank you."

"Ms. Benson, can I ask you a question?"

"Sure," I responded.

"Well, Adam sometimes acts funny—like he's thinking a lot, not saying anything even if I ask him something. He's a nice friend, but different."

"Well, Ben," responded Adam's mother, "Adam is a just a quiet boy, very smart but likes you too."

"Okay, Ms. Benson, that's okay. I know. Like the other day, when this car stopped by the sidewalk and asked Adam where the hospital was, and Adam just stood there. They asked him to get in and take them there because they might not find it on their own. It's really not that far I said to them, and they told me to hush up. Adam didn't say anything, so I pulled him away and the car drove off. Why do you think they wanted Adam to go with them, Ms. Benson?"

"I don't know, Ben, but I'll ask Adam when we see him. Don't fret, Ben, it'll be okay you'll see."

Just then, Adam came walking down the street, books in hand, stargazing as usual in his own little world.

"Adam, so how was school today?" I asked.

A nod was all I would get. Oh, Adam does talk at times but only if it interests him or he feels someone is listening. I think to myself, "What about those men in the car? Could they influence Adam to go with them? Adam was so innocent.

It was about 4:00 p.m. Now Adam and Ben were playing in the backyard. Charles came home early for him but a nice surprise. I explained what had happened to Adam and his friend.

He said, "It's time when they come by again, I will confront them and get to the bottom of all of this."

"Charles, please be careful."

"Anna, let me handle this, please."

CHAPTER 7

That night at dinner, everyone seemed—how would you say—preoccupied. There was a spooky feeling around the table and all knew not too ask the wrong questions about Adam, as mom and dad (especially mom) would jump in and protect Adam.

Poor Adam, God forbid we'd offend him. Charles pushed his chair back, stood up, and began to speak. "Adam, please go to your room, I will see you later."

When Adam was out of sight, and hearing Charles sat down again, asked Anna and the girls to please listen.

"A man came into my shop today and proceeded to offer me a proposal concerning Adam. He went on to say that he and others represented a "research medical group" trying to help children such as Adam who were suffering from mental disorders with little or no help with just ordinary medical help offered today."

"Don't you want for your son to get better and fit into today's society like normal children?" asked the stranger. Charles was stunned. He didn't respond.

"What in the hell are you asking? I don't understand what you're saying. Who are you people and are you doctors or what?" asked Charles. "Why are you so interested in our son? Please leave my store; I have nothing more to say to you."

"Oh, we'll leave, but we'll be back. This offer could be very beneficial to your family moneywise, and just think about poor Adam and how he'd be helped. One way or the other you'll see it our way, Charles, best you think about it."

"Out of my store," shouted Charles, "and do not come back or come near our home."

The stranger looked hard at Charles, hesitated, and as he was leaving, he turned and looked at Charles and said, "You've not seen the last of me and best you think hard about your decision giving up Adam. It'll be best for all. Trust me. We have other methods to achieve our goals."

Charles sat silent for a few minutes to collect his thoughts. "What to do? What to say to Anna? We couldn't do any more for Adam and most likely he's never get better. Please dear God, help me to make the right decision. Please."

CHAPTER 8

Morning came too soon. The nerve of someone trying to take our son away. No way, not over my dead body. The day was slow, and my mind was wandering. What if these men were truly trying to help Adam and in the interim helping us as a family financially in times that were tough to say the least.

Late that afternoon the two men that had approached me came into my shop. "Charles Benson, let's talk and you listen. Charles, you know the local 'hospital' has fallen on hard times as we all have. We've taken up space there and have made great success in rehabilitating young people with the same problems as Adam. Look at this way, Charles, you will be helping your son and your own family. Think man, think, Charles."

"I don't understand what you want with Adam. Please explain further."

"Let me introduce myself. My name is Dr. Shake and this is Dr. Bloom. You can call me henry. Have you ever heard of 'interaction bionic brain scan'? A modern day medical breakthrough with results well beyond our best expectations."

Charles responded, "I just don't know, and besides, I would have to talk with my wife, Dr. Shake."

"Charles, you know your wife will not agree, why bother?"

"I'm sorry you'll have to go now. I'm very busy."

I decided to go home early that day and discuss all that had happened. I arrived home to find Anna in the kitchen, sobbing.

"Anna," I said, "what's the matter, Anna?"

"I called you at the store, where were you? Charles?"

"I decided to come early. We have to talk. But, why are you crying, Anna?"

"Adam is late from school, Charles. Late from school, late from school."

"What do you mean, Anna?"

"Sarah and Rebecca went looking for him and that boy he hangs with told them he saw Adam talking to some men in a car, like the one Adam described."

"Dear god!" yelled Charles. "Anna, please stay here and the girls too. I'll be back. Anna."

"Where are you going?"

"I'll explain later."

Charles ran out the door and drove directly to the hospital. Walking up the steps of the hospital, he began praying that all was well with Adam. I approached the front nurse's desk to find no one was there to help me.

"Hello! Hello! Hello!" I yelled.

Just then, a very shabby looking man tapped me on the shoulder and asked what I was doing here.

"I'm looking for my son. You seen him?"

"Sorry, bud, I'm only the custodian. Charles."

"But where are the doctors and nurses?"

"Beats me, they're usually asleep, Charles. Asleep."

"What about the patients?"

"Patients. We only have three, and they're too old to care."

CHAPTER 9

Night had fallen, and a strange feeling had come over me. The custodian just simply disappeared, and there I was alone in a cold and damp old hospital, surrounded by marble walls and floors, and not knowing what my next move would be.

I started to wander down the hall looking for anyone: nurse, doctor, or patent to help me in my plight in trying to find my son, Adam. So quiet and cold I couldn't imagine anyone that was here for care; and just then I felt a very cold breeze surround me coming from an open door down the hallway.

I slowly walked toward the open door, and just before I reached it, a hand grabbed my shoulder. I turned and it was Dr. Shake and another man with him. Quite large in statue with dark eyes within, teeth made of metal standing there not uttering a word, as he was waiting for a command from Dr. Shake.

Was I scared? Does it snow in the winter? That and confused and desperate to locate Adam. They ushered me toward the open door and there on the slab was a body.

"God, no! Not Adam! Please, Dr. Shake."

"You're a nosey one, aren't you now, Charles Benson? And now, maybe you'll listen to what we have to say."

"Where's my son? I demand to know right now."

"You'll demand nothing," Dr. Shake responds, "nothing. As we're in charge now. Not you."

Dr. Shake instructs his assistant to take Charles to the basement and lock the door. As Charles was being taken to the basement, he glanced at the body on the table and was overcome with grief with what he saw. A male body. Not Adam lying there, cut to ribbons with his guts and brains on the table next to it.

"Dear Jesus, what is going on here?" he asked himself. Away with him and return to dispose of the body. Hurry, hurry before Dr. Bloom returns.

As I lay there in a dark, cold basement room, damp, and smelling of rotten garbage, and critters biting me all over — I had to get out. It was so quiet with only the sound of dripping water overhead.

Time passed, and I had fallen asleep only to be awakened by an elderly lady who looked in her eighties, with the little light from the doorway who just stood there, not saying a word.

"Please." I asked. "Help me get out of here."

"Oh," the old lady responded, "you'll never leave here and like me, in time, you'll see you have no choice. I'd like to sit with you if I could." As she locked the door behind her.

"We can be friends, can't we?"

CHAPTER 10

The old lady that had locked the door behind her just sat there staring at me like she hadn't seen another human in years. The night passed slowly, and all I could think about was getting out of this God-forsaken place.

I can't believe she was that quick locking the door. But where was the key? I waited until she fell asleep and slowly crawled over to where she was lying.

She had on an old-fashioned house dress which smelled like the local dump. What a nightmare this has turned out to be? Locked up down here, can't find my son, and I'm sure by now, Anna is beside herself wondering what had happened to me. There wasn't even a window in this room which means the avenue of escape was the door.

I slowly started to search the old lady for the key when I could see under the door a light come on and footsteps. Now, they stopped and the light went off. The old lady awoke, still half asleep looked around and then settled down again.

Then before I could resume looking for the key, the light on the other side of the door went and I could hear movement like someone dragging a body across the floor. Then, a thump.

Now, someone was putting a key in the door and slowly opened it. The light from an old hanging bulb swinging back and forth made it possible for me to see the shadow of a very large man just standing there with blood dripping from his hands. I had to make a move. Now or never.

I jumped to my feet, over the old lady, and hit the man standing there like I did back in my football days and as big as he was it took him by surprise and he hit the floor.

Out the door I went, down the hallway, up a winding staircase to the next floor, hoping it would lead me to the street. Oh no! There was the custodian by the door. Could he be trusted? I walked up to him as to ask him a question and hoping the door was not locked, turned and ran as fast as I could and praying the door was open.

We were only maybe fifteen feet way but it seemed like forever before I reached it. I hit the handle, and yes, it opened and out I went.

It was early morning, still dark, so where I was running to, I had no idea. Away from this place for sure. It was the back door and it led me into the woods behind the hospital. Through the woods I ran until I hit a dirt road. The moon was full, that was a blessing.

CHAPTER 11

Taking a breath, standing on the side of the dirt road, pondering what would be my next move. Even with the moonlight above, I had trouble trying to determine which way to go with only two choices to make, left or right.

Just then, I heard the sound of a car coming and wondered if this would be my way out. As the car approached I hesitated to flag them down with the fear they were from the hospital out looking for me. What to do? Run or take a chance? It was just ordinary folks but this late at night. God, help me!

I stepped back, off the side of the road, as to get a better look at the approaching car and who it might be and fell to the ground. I lay still as the vehicle stopped right where I had fallen.

"Don't move, Charles. Don't move," I quietly repeated to myself.

Two men got out of the car and slowly started walking toward where I was lying. My heart was pumping so hard I could hardly breathe. They stopped only maybe two or three feet from me and one false move I was dead.

It seemed like forever before they moved on. I waited until they got back into their car and drove off. I stayed on the ground for hours it seemed and then got up. Would the road be safe to find a way out? As I pondered what to do next and looked around not knowing what to do or where to go, I noticed a clearing at the base of the hill. I had earlier come down.

"That's odd," I thought. In the middle of the woods with more trees than you could count, this one area was clear of any trees.

The full moon shining bright above seemed to focus on that area as to bring attention to it and begging for me to investigate. It was weird, the feeling I had alone here in the woods by myself. "What's going on?" I asked.

The clearing was only maybe twenty-five feet away, and the size of the area about twenty by twenty feet flat, covered with fallen leaves. I walked into the middle and stood there.

As I started to walk around, all of a sudden, I sank into the ground like swallowing me up and grabbing the ground around me trying to stop my burial alive. I could only yell for help but who would hear me in these dark woods.

It seemed forever submerged in the earth when I heard sounds not far from where I was. I could hear voices; they were coming closer and closer and closer. The moon was gone.

CHAPTER 12

The clouds were moving now away from the moon and light from that moon started to shimmer its way through the trees below. At least with the dark night, I had a chance. I wouldn't be seen by whoever was out there.

Here I was stuck in the ground up to my chest and so afraid to make a move. All of a sudden the trees started to sway back and forth and the moonlight went in and out. It was an eerie feeling to say the least. The silence, except for the wind hitting the trees was deafening.

Just then I heard footsteps nearing where I was and prayed they would not find me.

All of a sudden I heard, "Hey, you! What the hell are you doing down there?" and looking up I saw two young men; and my first thought was maybe they could help me.

"Please grab my arms and get me out of here."

They pulled me out and lay me down on safe ground. These two men stood above me and I didn't know what to think. These weren't the same two men that I had seen earlier. "Who were they and what did they want? What were they doing here in the woods at night?' I ask myself.

"Hello, my name is Charles, and I need your help."

There was silence. Again, I ask them what they wanted from me.

"Shut up, old man," one of the men yelled as the other man leaned toward me as to help me up.

"Up on your feet and don't move, Charles."

"I don't understand what's going on here" as the other man struck Charles about the head and he fell.

"You're money to us, old man, and we're going to take you to the hospital and collect. Try and run and you're dead, which is no problem with who we are taking you to, Charles."

I had to make a move before they brought me back to the hospital and soon. Maybe, if I faked a heart attack it may slow them up. Maybe trying to bribe them might help. Bribe them. I'm lucky I had enough monies to feed my family. Lie to them –anything but not back to that place.

"Let's go back to the road," one man said. "Go. Let's go."

I assumed they had a car there or possibly would just escort me back to the hospital along the road. I started to think back on my school days and I was a pretty good runner. These young men would be a challenge, but I had to try.

Through the woods not far from the road timing was important. We reached the road, turned, hit the one across the face, kicked the other, and ran as fast as I could down the road.

Clouds, please be my cover, moon shine another night.

CHAPTER 13

I ran as fast as I could, not knowing where I was going or going to find at the end of the road. The two I left behind were startled which gave me a head start.

I needed a break sometime, somewhere, if I was ever going to see my family again. Adam then came to mind. Poor Adam, where in God's name could he have gone to? My thoughts now as I was running were of Anna and the children and what they might be thinking happened to me.

I slowed my pace and stopped for a minute to catch my breath. Just then I could faintly see ahead of me down the road automobile lights. I would not take any chances, so I ducked into the woods again and hid until the car went by. The car went by very slowly obviously looking for me. It seemed like eternity for that car to pass. I waited for a while and then resumed track back on the road to safety and where that would take me I did not know.

I must have walked for at least one good hour and knowing where I lived not to be too far from the hospital, I wondered how much further should I go. It was pitch-black, not a star in the sky, and clouds had covered the moon.

Eerie to say the least. I stepped into the woods again to rest and found a large oak tree to lie against. I dozed off for how long I did not know and was awakened by the sound of birds and awoke to see the sun peeking through trees so high above me. I never thought I would be so happy to see the early morning dawn as I did that morning.

Now, to get my bearings and find my way home. I started to walk down the road hoping it would lead to a main road when I heard a vehicle coming behind me. To hide now in the daylight would be more difficult, but I couldn't trust anyone at this point especially if I didn't know them.

I ran into the woods out of view and waited for the car to pass by. I heard it stopped. My heart dropped. I didn't move a muscle. I could hear the crackling of the ground cover and the sound got louder.

"Charles," I heard, "what are you doing out here?"

CHAPTER 14

I hesitated to answer. Was that someone calling to me—a friendly voice. At this point, I couldn't trust anyone.

"Charles," I kept hearing, "is that you man? I've come to help you." Then I heard what I wanted to hear, "Anna is so worried and sent me out to find you, Charles. Can you hear me?"

I decided to come out of hiding and confront whoever it might be. Oh, what a sight for sore eyes when it was my brother, Benjamin, standing there with a smile on his face, with open arms.

Ben, that's what they called him, looked at Charles and, not knowing what to say, simply asked, "What in the hell are you doing out here? With Anna home with the girls worried sick about you and of course, by the way, where is Adam, Charles?"

"Ben," I responded, "to explain right now why I came out, just forget about it for now and trust me and help me search for my son."

"Search where?" Ben asked Charles.

"The hospital. I'm sure they have him there, Ben."

"Charles, are you feeling okay?"

Charles responds very angrily, "Am I feeling okay? After all I went through trying to find my son? Apparently, you're the one who's not feeling too well, Ben."

"Charles, calm down and talk to me."

Charles takes a breath and proceeds to tell Benjamin what had occurred in the last, say, twelve hours or so, trying to find Adam. Ben was amazed and to say the least frightened listening to what Charles had to say.

"My God, man who knew, Charles? This is a nightmare for sure and I don't know what to do."

"Charles," Ben responds, don't worry I'm here for you and Adam and we will find him."

" I certainly hope so, Ben. I'm really at my wits end, Benjamin."

"Charles, do you want to go home first and see Anna and the girls? Charles?"

"I would love to do that but I have to go on until I find Adam, Ben."

"No problem, I understand, and I'm here for you. Charles."

"If we go back to the road and turn right, it should take us back to the hospital grounds, Ben."

"What then?" he asked Charles.

"I'll have to retrace my steps through the woods and try to enter the rear without being seen, Ben."

"What if they find us and like what happened to you? Lock us up, Charles?"

"If we don't do anything and Adam is locked up in there then what, Ben?"

"I don't know, Charles. I really don't know."

Ben and headed down the road toward the hospital; it was full daylight by now and worrying if we'd be seen, crossed my mind. God help us.

CHAPTER 15

As we were walking along the road to the hospital, Ben turned to me and asked, "Charles, shouldn't we go back home first and see if Adam returned home?"

"I really don't know what to do, Ben . . . that's my problem." We walked for a while, and then it hit me. What if Adam was safe, and we walk into the hospital and can't get out. We decided to turn around and return home. I'm sure Anna and the girls would be waiting with open arms. We walked for about ten minutes when we heard a car coming and not taking any chances that it might be them who were looking for us. We ran into the woods and lay there still and quiet as a church mouse holding our breath for dear life. All of a sudden, the car stopped, and two men got out. They seemed to be walking around the car looking at the road. Would they spot our footprints in the dirt? God help us. It seemed like eternity, and finally, they got back into the car and proceeded toward the hospital. We waited for about five minutes and then resumed our way home.

After about another ten or fifteen minutes, we saw the main road ahead. From there, home was just about another ten minutes or less. Just a few minutes into our walk, we heard another car coming from behind.

"Charles . . ." Ben yelled. "I'm going to stop this car, and if it's them, it's time we confront them and get to the bottom of this mess."

"Ben, please don't get involved. These are dangerous people, and if something happens to us, what good are we going to be to Adam?"

"Sorry, Charles, but enough is enough." And at that point, he attempted to wave the vehicle down.

"Ben . . . watch out!" I said as I could see the car starting to skid. I ran to Ben to get him out of the way when all of a sudden the car hit him, and he fell to the ground. The car stopped, and two men and a woman got out to help. No, they weren't from the hospital. Thank god. The driver of the car looked at me and asked, "Why would he jump in front of my car?"

"I feel so sorry. What can we do?" he asked. The woman with them quickly suggested we get him to a hospital. "We'll take him, sir, in our car rather than wait for an ambulance. Sir, where's the hospital?"

CHAPTER 16

Charles at that moment turned to Ben, and they both just stared at eachother. "Go back to that hospital."

"I don't think so," Charles beckoned to Ben. "Ben, we can't go back to that hospital under these circumstances," stated Charles. "We'll just tell these people you are not badly hurt, and we'll take care of it later."

"Yes, good idea."

"Sir, do you have a minute?"

" We are very appreciative for the offer of taking my brother to the hospital, but we will wait as I don't think he is seriously injured."

"No," responded one of the other men in the car. "We'll have none of that. Your brother must be attended to."

"No, really," Charles responded back.

They went back and forth, and finally, the other man said to Charles, "Don't worry about the cost of any treatment. My brother works there, and maybe you know him. His name is Dr. Shake."

At this point, Charles looked at Ben, and they couldn't believe what they have just heard. Now we know we're not going. Just then, the ambulance pulled up. The door to the ambulance opened and at the steps was Dr. Shake's assistant.

"So what do we have here?" the assistant looked at Charles and Ben and said, "Isn't this so fortunate that we meet again? There is some unfinished business back at the hospital, which we can take care of after we fix you up, Ben. Aren't you the lucky one? Now, watch your step getting in. We wouldn't want for anything to happen to you."

On the ride to the hospital, Charles turned to Ben, and both agree this is one hospital stay we'll really regret. Just then, the assistant turned around to Charles and said, "By the way, your son Adam is in good hands, and soon you'll be too."

Charles then knew it's now or never and must return to the hospital. The ride to the hospital didn't take long, and soon they arrived and met at the door by Dr. Shake and Dr. Bloom. "Welcome back, Charles! We so missed you. Would you like to see your son Adam? He's in recovery."

At this point, Charles yelled out, "You bastard! What have you done to our son?"

Ben jumped in and attempted to strike Dr. Shake and was immediately restrained by the assistant and taken away leaving Charles behind. Dr. Shake said, "Listen, Charles, we'll take good care of your brother."

CHAPTER 17

They placed me in a room by myself, and it seemed forever before someone came to the door. "Charles?" a voice rang out. "Are you in there? Charles, answer me."

At this point, I was afraid to answer, and it didn't sound like Ben or Adam.

"Who are you?" I yelled.

A few minutes passed, and the door opened. I placed myself in the rear of the room, in the far corner and really not knowing what to do or react. The room was dark, and the only light was from the adjoining room which was only visible when the door opened. The door opened and in walked a very large man, who just stood there saying nothing.

"Who are you, and where is my son?"

"I'm here to help you," answered the man. "I'm the custodian"

"Why would you help me, and why should I trust you?" Charles responded.

"Let me talk to you, and I will explain. I've been here for most of my life and have not been treated well . . .not well at all."

"Maybe we can help each other, but we have to trust each other as well."

"Yes, I agree," replied the custodian.

"By the way, what is your name?"

The custodian replies, "My name is Jake, and I don't have a last name. I was born here in this hospital many years ago. Oh, maybe forty or so, and I have only been living outside with aunt and uncle for about three years and then they died and here I am. I guess forever. Mr. Charles, I want to tell you I saw your son, and he's okay, and he spoke to me. He asked for you and his mother, but I didn't know what to say.

"That's okay, Jake. I understand. Right now we have find a way to locate my son and brother and out of here. Would you be willing come along with us?"

"Oh yes, I would, sir. Oh yes, I would."

Now comes the hard part trying to find Adam and Ben without being caught.

Charles asked Jake, "Remember, these are very evil people who will do anything to get their way.

"I understand," said Jake.

"Thanks, Jake."

"Charles, I know this place like the back of my hand. I will help you in any way I can. There are dungeons beneath the first floor which lead to the outside. There is very little or no light, so we have to get some flashlights. The supply closet is locked up with a big paddle lock, and it won't be easy. Charles, hey, we'll give a go. What do we have to lose at this time?"

"Prayers, Jake. Do you pray?"

"I sure do, but so far they haven't been answered."

"Patience, Jake, patience, and in due time god will answer our needs. Trust me."

Just then, the sound of footsteps interrupted us.

"Charles, lie down. I'll handle this."

CHAPTER 18

As Charles lay there on the floor, Jake awaited for who might be at the door. A voice from the other side yelled. "Who's in there? Show yourself."

Jake quickly opened the door so not to arouse any suspicions. Standing there was the doctor's assistant by the name of Rodney or better known to the staff as the enforcer and mean to the bone. Not the sharpest knife in the draw but loyal to Dr. Bloom and Dr. Shake.

"What are you doing here?" asked Rodney.

"I was checking on the 'new guest' we have. You know, to make sure he's comfortable."

"Oh, yes," Rodney responded thinking he knows what's going on. "By the way, Dr. Bloom wants you to bring this guy upstairs to the exam room." "Now!" he shouted. "Right now!"

"Okay. Okay," Jake answered. "We'll be right there. Go, we're okay, and tell the doctor we're coming."

"Charles, he's gone. Come and follow me."

"Where are we going?" asks Charles.

Jake responded, "We are going to find a way out of here, and when we do, I'm going with you. Is this okay with you Charles?"

Charles said, "You get me and my son out of here, and you can live with us, and I mean that."

"Thank you, Charles. I thank you for that. Now, follow me, and don't make a sound. We will be going down a long ramp way along the sewer system which eventually will lead to the outer grounds.

Unfortunately, we are on the other side of the hospital, and there are no lights along the way and it is infested with rats and other creatures.

Charles asked, "You seemed nervous."

"Oh no, Charles. I just love walking along 'rats' and other creatures . . . joking. I'll make it." We started down a corridor, which Jake explained would lead us to the ramp way and then the outside. But first, I explained to Jake that we cannot leave here without Adam.

Jake said, "We'll find your son. Trust me." And he proceeded on. Between the rats and spiders, I was at my wit's end. It seemed forever, and finally, we reached the outer door.

Now to back track and locate Adam. "Jake . . ." I asked. "Where do you think my son could be?"

"Just trust me, and do as I say."

We backtracked about half the way we had gone, and at that point, Jake shouted to stop. "Be quiet! I'm looking for a door which will hopefully lead us to the upper level and then to the exam rooms where your son is." Jake started to feel around the outer walls for a door. It's been years since I've been down here. Feeling around, I felt a padlock. Not good.

CHAPTER 19

Jake and I ventured further down until we came upon another door, and it was not locked.

"Jake, I'll go through and let you know what I find."

It was eerie dark on the other side, and not knowing where it would lead me was frightening in itself. I kept feeling pipes along the walls. Finally, I came to an opening completely round in shape and decided to crawl in to see where it may take me. It seemed to me it was unused sewer pipe with smaller pipes along the sides, which possibly carried water or for drainage. The fit was tight, but I proceeded anyway, hoping it would lead to some part of the hospital and then to Adam and my brother Ben. After about ten minutes crawling along rats and spiders, I finally spotted some light at the end of the tunnel. *Oh,* I thought to myself, *what about Jake? I certainly could not go back for him. Let's hope he follows me.* I'm now at the end, and I find what appears to be small metal bars covering the opening. Please give me the strength to push through. Lying there, I'm trying to figure how I can turn myself around so I can use my feet to push it out. I can't turn around. Dam it. I start to push it with my hands to no avail. Now, to make things even worse, I can feel a rat nibbling on my shoe. I kick it way, and it's back. Dear Lord, give me the power to overcome this. Just then, I hear Jake coming toward me, and maybe the two of us can together force it open.

"Charles, hold still. I'm just a few feet behind you."

Charles explained the situation, and together with brute strength; it opened. It led into another stoned passageway damp, no lights, and more rats. We were then wading through about a foot of water and sewage and not even knowing how far we'd have to go or where it would lead us. We both were very tired and decided to take a break.

"Jake, I hear voices, and it sounds like it from above us."

We come to the end, and it splits . . . right or left. Lord, please help us.

CHAPTER 20

At this point, we really did not have too many choices. The bad guys are above us, and there is really no place for us to go. Charles whispers to Jake, "We will have wait it out."

"Gee thanks, Charles! Tell that to the rats."

Approximately one hour goes by, and there's silence.

Charles asked Jake, "What say you, right or left?"

Jake replied, "It's a crap shoot. Does it really matter anymore?"

Charles said, "We'll go right."

Now the next tunnel was the better of the two. We crawled through not too far, and at the end came upon a room liken to a pump house. We entered and it was dark like the black cat of the night. We decided to relax for a while and determine our next move. There were no sound or voices—a good thing. We searched around and found a door. Where would it lead, only God would know. Oh yes, God we're praying.

"Listen, Jake, it's best we take a chance and try and open it as it may lead us to the main house."

"I'm not familiar with this part of the house, but it can't be too far from the hospital, where most likely your son and brother are. Think positive, Charles. We've come this far and not for nothing. So very carefully we opened the door which led us to a long hall with rooms a long way. I think I remember this hallway vaguely but not sure as we weren't permitted to wonder into the family quarters by ourselves."

As we quietly walked down the hallway, we heard footsteps coming our way.

"Here, Jake, in this room! The door is unlocked."

We entered the room and the lights went on, and there to greet us was Rodney the enforcer. "Gentlemen, we have waiting for you. I'm sure Dr. Shake will be surprised and amused. Oh, by the way your son and brother are well at least for the time being. Just to let you know that when we start our experiments on them . . . guess what . . . you can watch. Dr. Shake and Dr. Bloom just love an audience, and they don't even charge admission. All that crawling around, sneaking around, and guess who you find. I feel we have an attraction to each other. Don't you?"

CHAPTER 21

Now in that same room that Charles and Jake have entered and not knowing Rodney was waiting, there was also a patient who was catatonic and was just lying there on his bed. He was probably middle aged, very thin, and obviously not being fed. He looked startled that no one enters this room except for Rodney, the enforcer. This is what they call the waiting room where Charles' son and brother were before entering the room of horrors two doors down. Charles leans toward Jake with a plan of some kind maybe attempting to distract Rodney and get the hell out of there and find his son and brother. Well, as we were pondering the situation, the patient, laying on the bed, bolted up knocking Rodney to the floor and then motions us to get the hell out of there.

"Yes, but where do we go?"

"Out we go and on the other side of the hallway and other room, which we hope is empty."

We quietly enter the room and find more patients there, who are apparently awaiting the same fate as my son and brother. "No, we can't stay here too long. What the heck to do? We know on the other side about two rooms further down is where my son and brother are being held by Dr. Shake and Dr. Bloom. Their fate . . . what is their fate?"

Charles turns to Jake and says, "We have to take a chance and force our way into that room hoping it's where they are being held captive. Dear Lord, be with us."

The time has come; no turning back. We are too close to try hiding and more thinking. "Let's do it."

As we left the room, I noticed a fire extinguisher on the wall across the other side of the hallway. That's it; I yelled to Jake. "I'll grab it, and you open the door, the one where we are hoping they're in."

Talk about a gamble and the odds not that great.

"Well, Jake, are you ready?"

"Let's do it!" And with that, Jake opened the door, and we were confronted by the two doctors. There, lying on operating tables, were Adam and Ben, and they were certainly a sight for sore eyes. Dr. Shake and Dr. Bloom were . . . you might say a bit surprised. Jake grabbed an instrument off a table, and I sprayed both as they were fairly close. They were blinded at that point, and Jake slashed the one doctor. I hit the other one over the head with the fire extinguisher, and he dropped to the floor. The other doctor, attempting to run through the door, ran into Rodney like we need him right now. I sprayed them both and yelled to Jake, "Grab a knife or whatever and stab them both as they were both rubbing their eyes from the foam I sprayed on them." It worked and he stabbed them and they were bleeding. We removed the restraints off Adam and Ben and proceeded out the door. Just then, the first patient, who helped us get away from Rodney, yelled from down the hallway, "Please take me with you!" Without hesitation as I helped Adam and Ben, Jake took the patient by the arm, and we ran like hell looking for a door leading to the outside. Finally, we came to a very large door, and it had to be an exit. It was locked, but my brother Ben, who worked years back for a locksmith, needed very little time to open and old door such as this was. We were finally out and headed for the road leading out to the main road—homeward bound. God is good. As we walked along the dirt road, we kind of almost started laughing looking back at what we all have thought. Relieved. Do bears like honey—yeah. It took about one hour before we finally reached the main road into town. Just then, a friend, who frequented my store, spotted us, and the rest is history. At home relaxing with my family and of course Jake and after notifying the authorities regarding what happened, I turned to my wife. "Hey, what's for supper? But first, a bottle of fine twelve-year scotch has preference and would you join me the boys, and Adam what you're now eighteen?"

"Well, I think Mom wouldn't mind."

"No, Charles, I wouldn't mind at all."

ABOUT THE AUTHOR

Daniel J Costello is the author of *The Penny Doctors* and resides in Central Florida with his wife. He has two sons, five grandchildren, and one great-grandchild. After starting work at a young age (1940s) and having succeeded at several careers, one of them as an NYPD police officer, he now retired. After coming from a large Irish family living on Long Island, New York, town of Hicksville third generation, he has many stories to tell. His plan for a new career is to succeed as a writer. He has given up his passion for golf in order to write.